KRYPTO THE SUPERDOG
SUPERPET!

by Michael Anthony Steele
Art by Min S. Ku and David Tanguay

SCHOLASTIC INC.

New York   Toronto   London   Auckland   Sydney
Mexico City   New Delhi   Hong Kong   Buenos Aires

ISBN 0-439-72507-0

Published by Scholastic Inc. SCHOLASTIC and associated logos are trademarks
and/or registered trademarks of Scholastic Inc.

12 11 10 9 8 7 6 5 4 3 2 1   6 7 8 9 10/0

Printed in the U.S.A.
First printing, March 2006

Hi! My name is Krypto. I'm just an average dog, living a regular dog's life.

Okay, so maybe I'm not an average dog.

But I still do regular dog things!

Just like other dogs, I have my own family.
My best friend is a boy named Kevin.

We have lots of fun together!
"Great catch, Krypto!" shouts Kevin.

Just like other dogs, I like to play at the park!

Kevin and I always have a good time.
"Wow!" shouts Kevin. "Look how high my kite can go!"

At night, I protect our house, just like
regular dogs. What was that noise?

No burglar is getting in while I'm on duty.
I am one super guard dog!

And just like other dogs,
I enjoy sniffing around for buried treasure!

Then I dig, dig, dig, dig, DIG!
"What are you doing, Krypto?" asks Kevin.

I like to chew on bones, just like other dogs.

And just like other dogs, I can get into trouble sometimes.
"You're not supposed to chew on dinosaur bones," says Kevin.

Okay, so maybe I'm not like other dogs.

I live in a place called Metropolis.
It's a city full of people, and sometimes people need help.
Oh no! That giant wrecking ball is falling!

"It's a bird!" cries a construction worker.
"It's a plane!" yells another construction worker.
"It's Superdog!" shouts a third construction worker.

Being Superdog is hard work.
In a big city like Metropolis, there is always someone
who needs help.

I always do the best I can!
I enjoy helping people, just like Superman.

Being Superdog is a lot of fun.
But I enjoy being Superpet even more!